Night Tree

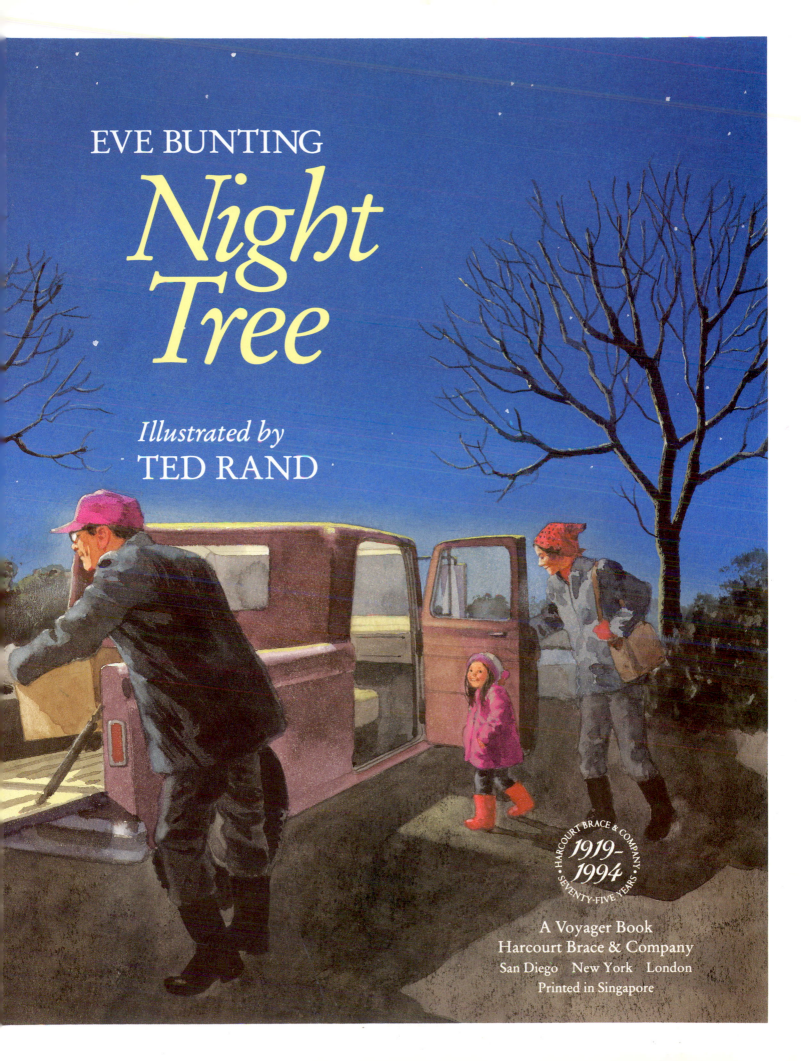

EVE BUNTING

Night Tree

Illustrated by
TED RAND

A Voyager Book
Harcourt Brace & Company
San Diego   New York   London
Printed in Singapore

On the night before Christmas we always go to find our tree. We bundle up so we're warm. Nina is already wearing her boots that are too big for her. She has been wearing them all day.

Dad sets our box in the back of the truck with the rest of his stuff and the four of us squish into the front seat.

We drive through the bright Christmas streets to where the dark and quiet begin.

Nina is almost asleep in Mom's lap when we stop.

"Are we there?" I ask, and Dad says "Yes" and rolls down the
windows so we can smell the tree smell.

We scramble out.

There are oaks growing here and alder and maples that are
bare now and white in the moonshine. The pines and the
spruces and the firs are green.

This is called Luke's Forest, but Dad says it's not really a forest, just a nice forgotten place where our town ends.

Dad goes first on the path between the trees, carrying our box and the big red lantern.

Mom and Nina go next, holding hands.

I come last, with the blanket.

It hasn't snowed yet. It's so cold my breath hurts.
The sky is spattered with stars, and the moon, big as a
basketball, slides in and out between the treetops.

Dad's lantern sweeps ahead.

"Look," he whispers.

We stop.

A deer is watching us. I see the brightness of its eyes; then it
turns and it's gone.

"Here's our tree," Dad says.

It has been our tree forever and ever. We walk around it, touching it.

"It's grown since last year," I say.

Mom puts her hand on my shoulder. "So have you."

"So have I," Nina says. Nina hates to be left out.

An owl hoots, deep in the darkness.
There are secrets all around us.

"Can I put on the popcorn chain?" Nina asks. She hops up and down and right out of one of her boots. Mom helps her get it back on.

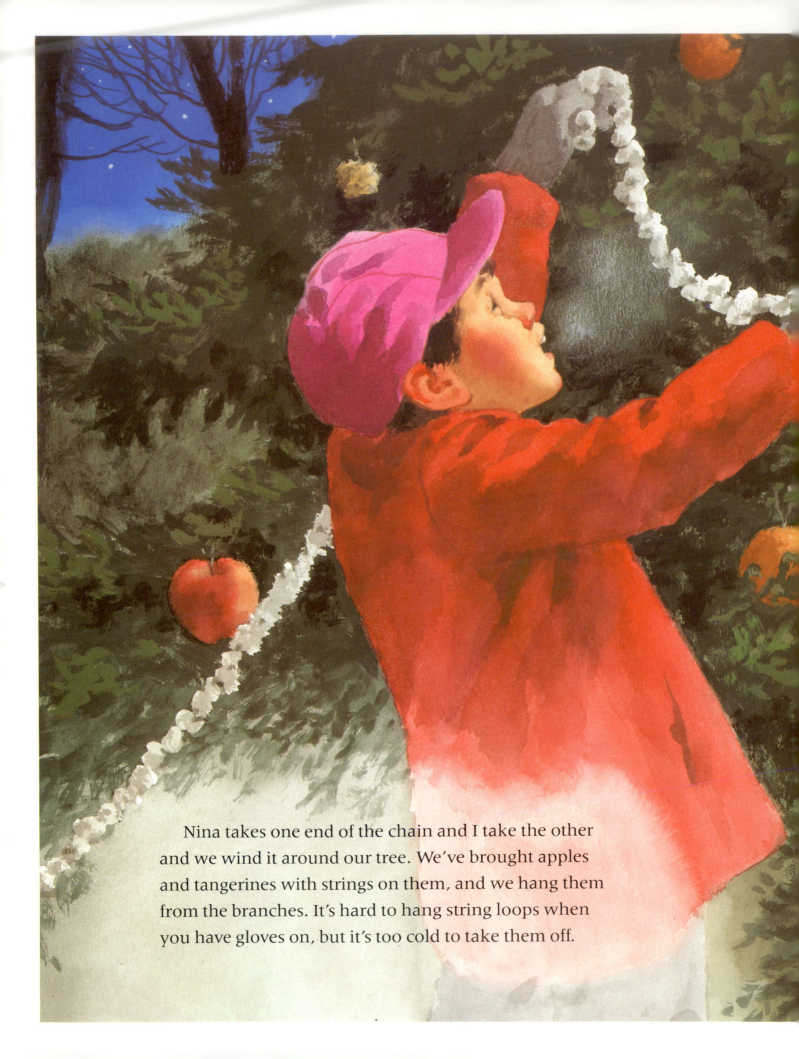

Nina takes one end of the chain and I take the other
and we wind it around our tree. We've brought apples
and tangerines with strings on them, and we hang them
from the branches. It's hard to hang string loops when
you have gloves on, but it's too cold to take them off.

For weeks we've been making balls of sunflower seeds
and pressed millet and honey. We hang those, too.
    We scatter shelled nuts and breadcrumbs and pieces of apple
underneath for the little creatures who can't climb very well.
    Our tree looks so pretty.

Mom says I should spread the blanket so we can sit and admire our tree. She has brought a thermos of hot chocolate. I take off my gloves and toast my hands around my warm cup.

Dad turns off the lantern and we stay quiet, hoping some of the little animals will come while we're here, hoping the deer will come back. But it doesn't.

"It's shy," Dad says. "I'm shy, too," Nina tells him.

Before we leave she and I get to choose a Christmas
carol to sing. I choose "Oh Come, all ye Faithful."
Nina chooses "Old MacDonald Had a Farm."
"That's not a Christmas song, silly," I tell her, but Mom says it's
fine and a very nice song, too.
We sing fast because there are a lot of verses and it's getting colder.

After the last "E-I-O" we gather up our things and head for the truck.

I look back once.

Our tree has folded itself into the darkness, but I think I can see it still, stars caught in its branches and the moon swinging lopsided on top.

Nina gets tired and Dad has to wrap her in the blanket and carry her. I carry her boots.

Later, in bed, I think about our tree, and sometimes, next day, when the aunts and the uncles and the cousins are at our house and it's noisy and happy, I let my mind go back to Luke's Forest. I think of the birds having Christmas dinner and the squirrels and the opossums and the raccoons and the skunks.

There might even be a bear because Dad says bears don't really sleep all winter and if one's going to wake up I just bet it would wake up for Christmas.

Maybe a fox has come, stepping high on its thin, sharp paws, and they're all there together, singing their own Christmas songs on Christmas Day around our tree.

To Anna Eve,
our palindrome girl
— E. B.

To Bill Martin Jr,
who is responsible for
my being an illustrator
of children's books
— T. R.

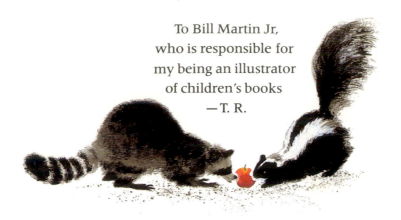

Library of Congress Cataloging-in-Publication Data
Bunting, Eve, 1928–
Night tree/by Eve Bunting; illustrated by Ted Rand.—1st ed.
p.   cm.
Summary: A family makes its annual pilgrimage to decorate an evergreen
tree with food for the forest animals at Christmastime.
ISBN 0-15-201030-0
[1. Trees—Fiction. 2. Forest animals—Fiction. 3. Christmas—Fiction.
4. Family life—Fiction.] I. Rand, Ted, ill. II. Title.
PZ7.B91527Ni   1991
[E]—dc20   90-36178

Special Edition for Scholastic Book Fairs, Inc.

A B C D E

Printed in Singapore

The illustrations in this book were done in traditional watercolors with the
addition of chalk and grease pencil on Crescent illustration board.
The display type was set in Stempel Garamond.
The text type was set in Meridien.
Composition by Thompson Type, San Diego, California
Color separations were made by Bright Arts, Ltd., Singapore.
Printed and bound by Tien Wah Press, Singapore
Production supervision by Warren Wallerstein and Ginger Boyer
Designed by Lydia D'moch